PLEASE WASH
YOUR HANDS
BEFORE YOU READ ME
AND KEEP ME CLEAN

Who Was It?

Marissa Moss

Houghton Mifflin Company

Boston   1989

For Mom

Library of Congress Cataloging-in-Publication Data

Moss, Marissa.
    Who was it? / Marissa Moss.
        p.   cm.
    Summary: After Isabelle breaks the cookie jar, she and her brother
Jerome invent a variety of wild stories to explain the damage to
their mother.
    ISBN 0-395-49699-3
    [1. Honesty—Fiction.   2. Parent and child—Fiction.]   I. Title.
PZ7.M8535Wh   1989   88-30354
[E]—dc19   CIP
                                         AC

Printed in the United States of America

Y 10 9 8 7 6 5 4 3 2 1

Who Was It?

"Want a cookie?" Isabelle asked.

"But it's not cookie time," said Jerome.

And CRASH! went the cookie jar.

"You're in trouble now!" said Jerome.

Mama opened the kitchen door. "Who made this horrible mess?"

"It wasn't me!" said Isabelle.

"It wasn't me!" said Jerome.

"Then who was it?" asked Mama, looking straight at Isabelle.

"It was a fire-breathing dragon!" said Isabelle. "He didn't even bother to open the cookie jar. He smashed it on the floor and licked up the cookies with his long red tongue."

"A dragon?" Mama asked. "How could anything so big get in here?"

"Well, it wasn't *that* big, but it was big," said Isabelle. "It was a big, furry monster."

"He squeezed through the window, grabbed the cookie jar, and threw it on the floor."

"A big, furry monster? I didn't think you believed in monsters anymore," said Mama.

"Well, it was big and furry," said Isabelle. "It was two big, furry kangaroos who escaped from the zoo. Their stomachs started to growl, 'We want cookies!

Cookies now!' 'Me first!' said one kangaroo. '*Me* first!'
said the other, and they pulled at the cookie jar until it
fell through their paws and crashed on the floor."

"Hmmm," said Mama. "I haven't heard of any
kangaroos loose in this neighborhood. And do kangaroos
even like cookies?"

"Well, it was someone who liked cookies," Isabelle
said. "Someone from this neighborhood, too. It was an
enormous, cookie-loving dog with eyes as big as saucers."

"He jumped through the window and wolfed down some cookies before he ran.away to chase after Mrs. Ramira's cat."

"Well," said Mama, "first it was a dragon, then a
monster, then two kangaroos, and now an enormous,
saucer-eyed dog. Who would you say it was, Jerome?"

Jerome looked at Isabelle. Isabelle looked at Jerome.

"Well," Jerome said. "Maybe it was a homesick astronaut just back from the moon who was very hungry for cookies."

23

"No, Jerome," said Isabelle. "Maybe it wasn't an astronaut. Maybe it wasn't an enormous dog, or two kangaroos, or a monster, or a dragon, either."

"Maybe it was one hungry little kid who just wanted
one cookie when CRASH! went the cookie jar."

"One hungry little kid?" asked Mama.

"One hungry little girl," said Isabelle.

"One hungry little girl?" asked Mama.

Jerome looked at Isabelle. Isabelle looked at the floor.

"Me," she said.

"Ohhh," said Mama.

"Yes," said Isabelle.
"But I'll help clean up this mess
and bake new cookies."
"Me, too," said Jerome.

29

"What about the dragon, the big, furry monster, the kangaroos, and the saucer-eyed dog?" Mama asked. "Do you think they'll ever come back?"

"Don't worry," said Isabelle. "They won't. From now on our cookies will be safe."

"Unless," said Jerome, "it's cookie time."